Dino Corp

First published by Allen & Unwin in 2018

Allen & Unwin
83 Alexander Street
Crows Nest NSW 2065
Australia
Phone: (61 2) 8425 0100
Email: info@allenandunwin.com
Web: www.allenandunwin.com

A Cataloguing-in-Publication entry is
available from the National Library of Australia
www.trove.nla.gov.au

ISBN 978 1 76029 604 9

For teaching resources, explore
www.allenandunwin.com/resources/for-teachers

Cover and text design by Sandra Nobes
Set in 16 pt ITC Stone Informal by Sandra Nobes
This book was printed in November 2017 at
McPherson's Printing Group, Australia.

1 3 5 7 9 10 8 6 4 2

macparkbooks.com

MIX
Paper from
responsible sources
FSC® C001695

The paper in this book is FSC® certified.
FSC® promotes environmentally responsible,
socially beneficial and economically viable
management of the world's forests.

D-BOT SQUAD

BOOK 8
Dino Corp

MAC PARK

Illustrated by JAMES HART

ALLEN&UNWIN
SYDNEY • MELBOURNE • AUCKLAND • LONDON

Chapter One

Hunter, Ethan and Charlie were worried. They were in the sky on their triple d-bot. Below, three huge T-rexes were moving in on one triceratops.

'Growl! Roar!'

'Growl!' Rumble!

Boom! 'Growl!'

'If we don't do something, that tops will be eaten!' cried Ethan.

'We can't just ray the T-rexes now, though,' said Charlie. 'They're too close to that tops. We might teleport it away too. Then we couldn't stop them eating it.'

'And we can't help it here until we fix our d-bots,' said Ethan.

'This triple d-bot is no match for three T-rexes,' Hunter agreed.

Hunter thought calmly.

'Hmm. This is hard.'

Hunter scratched his head.

'How can we get the T-rexes away from the tops? A T-rex will get us with its tail before we can get close. And even if we got close, its arms could head-lock us.'

'T-rexes work well as a team,
too,' added Ethan.

'Yes, but so do we!' cried Charlie.
'I know we can do this.'

'What if we think another way?'
said Hunter. 'We're thinking of
how T-rexes can hurt us. What
about how they can help us?'

'But how?' Ethan asked.

'Well, a T-rex is a really caring parent...' Hunter said.

A slow smile spread over Charlie's face. 'T-rexes always look after their eggs! They never leave them alone.'

'Exactly,' said Hunter. 'If we had a nest of T-rex eggs, they'd go to it. They'd leave the tops alone.'

Ethan grabbed an egg-box
from behind him on his d-bot.
He turned on the X-ray torch
on its side. 'I can help with
that,' he said. 'Look!'

'Yes, T-rex eggs!' cried Hunter.

'Will a T-rex look after any T-rex egg?' asked Ethan.

'And what if the eggs start to hatch?' wondered Charlie.

'**Rooooooaaaaarrr.**'

'We're about to find out,' said Hunter.

Chapter Two

The three T-rexes moved in
even closer. The tops was totally
trapped.

'We're almost too late,' Charlie
cried. 'Time to make a plan!'

1. Change the d-bots.
2. Make three T-rex nests.
3. Fly the eggs near the T-rexes' noses.
sniff
4. Lead them to the nests.

'We'll need those eggs super close to the dinos' noses,' said Hunter.

'If they smell them, they'll probably smell us too,' said Ethan. 'Either way, they'll chase us.'

'And T-rexes are fast,' said Charlie. 'So we'll need to fly fast too. Our triple d-bot needs to become three super-speedy d-bots.'

'What about the two broken wings?' asked Hunter. 'We can't get new ones.'

'I have an idea,' said Ethan. 'Charlie, can you help me? Hunter, you build the nests.'

'I know lots about T-rex nests,' Hunter said. 'They were really long.'

'Okay, team, let's go!' said Charlie.

They landed in a clearing
nearby. Charlie and Ethan
began work on the d-bots.
Hunter found a good spot, with
lots of open space. Then he dug
three long nests.

Here goes, thought Hunter. *This
plan had better work!*

He raced back to Charlie and
Ethan.

Hunter saw what the others had built. 'Wow, chopper d-bots!' he said. Ethan and Charlie grinned.

'We can carry the eggs in these tail-bags,' said Ethan. 'The smell will get through the netting.'

'And these extend-o-tails can grow longer,' added Charlie.

'Awesome!' said Hunter.

They placed a dino-egg
carefully into each tail-bag.

'Ready, D-Bot Squad?' Hunter
called. 'Let's go and save that
tops!'

They flew back towards the
three T-rexes and the tops.

'**Rooooooaaaaarrr!**'

'**Rooooooaaaaarrr!**'

'**Rooooooaaaaarrr!**'

'**Screeeeeeeeeeeek!**'

'That sounds bad,' cried Hunter.
'I hope we're not too late!'

Chapter Three

The team hovered above the
dinos. Below, the tops was lying
on the ground. It was hemmed
in by the three T-rexes. It had
been hurt.

'Oh, no!' said Charlie. 'The tops has a big cut on its leg.'

'Poor tops,' said Ethan.

One T-rex nudged the tops with its huge head. The tops didn't move. It was too hurt.

'No!' yelled Hunter. 'Leave it alone!'

Hunter swooped closer to the dinos. His tail-bag trailed over the T-rex's head.

The T-rex kept nudging the tops. It ignored the egg.

'Come on,' Hunter called. He made his d-bot tail longer. 'Smell this!'

He swooped again. This time, the tail-bag almost touched the T-rex's nose. It looked up.

Sniff! Snort!

'It's working, Hunter!' cried
Ethan. 'It's smelling the egg.'

For a moment, Hunter hovered
as steadily as he could. Then
he flew slowly towards the nests.

Follow me, he thought. *Come
after your egg.*

The T-rex took a step away
from the tops. Then it followed
hot on Hunter's tail. Hunter
flew faster.

Stomp! Stomp! Stomp!

'Let's go,' Ethan said to Charlie.
They made their tails longer
and swooped in. Their tail-bags
passed under the huge noses of
the other T-rexes.

The other T-rexes lifted their
heads.

Sniff! Snort!

Sniff! Snort!

'I sure hope they'll follow us too,' Charlie said. She moved away from her T-rex. The dino turned. It followed Charlie and her egg.

Ethan took a deep breath. 'Your turn, rexy,' he said.

Ethan took off. The T-rex was right behind him.

Ethan zipped along beside Charlie. The two giant T-rexes stomped behind them. Their heads pointed towards the eggs in the tail-bags.

'Look, Hunter's doing zigzags. It's so we can catch up,' Charlie said. 'Hurry!'

They all reached the nests together. 'Yay, team!' Hunter cried. 'We did it.'

'Now to drop the eggs into the nests,' Ethan said.

'Careful,' said Charlie. 'We'll have to go low for this.'

The team swooped down over Hunter's three nests. 'Go!' Hunter cried.

They pushed a button on their remotes. Their d-bot tail-bag nets opened. One egg rolled into each nest.

Stomp! Stomp! Stomp!

Stomp! Stomp! Stomp!

Stomp! Stomp! Stomp!

'Fly up!' Charlie shouted.
'Up, up, up!'

The team sped to safety, high above the nests. They held their breath as the T-rexes sniffed at the nests.

I hope they don't stomp all over the eggs!' said Charlie.

'Look after your babies,' Ethan said softly.

The T-rexes stomped around the eggs. Then, slowly and gently, they sat on them.

'Phew!' Hunter said.

'Wow, just look at them,' cried Charlie. 'They've gone all soft and gooey!'

'They're so big, yet so gentle,' said Hunter.

'Uh-oh!' Ethan said. He pointed to one of the nests. 'Something is happening to the egg under Hunter's T-rex.'

'That egg's starting to hatch,'
Charlie said, her eyes wide.

Crack! Crickle! Crickle! **Crack!**

One leg shot out of the egg.
Then a little arm broke free.

Crack! Crickle! Crickle! **Crack!**

'Another one's cracking,' Ethan
cried. 'They're hatching so fast!'

'Quickly!' Hunter said. 'We need to ray the T-rexes before the eggs totally hatch. Those babies will be on the move soon.'

Hunter flew to one side of the nests. Ethan flew to the other. Charlie flew over the middle nest.

'Three, two, one...now!' Charlie called.

The team hit the teleport buttons on their d-bands. In a second, the T-rexes and the eggs were gone.

'Now to help that tops,' said Hunter. 'Let's go.'

The tops still hadn't moved, except to roll over. It was breathing strangely.

'It's okay,' Hunter said softly. He stroked its belly. 'We'll help you.'

'I'll call Ms Stegg,' said
Charlie. 'She'll know what to
do.' She pressed the talk button
on her d-band.

'Good work, team,' said Ms Stegg.
'You kept the tops safe.'

'But how can we help the tops now?' asked Ethan.

'Don't worry,' said Ms Stegg. 'We'll look after it when it gets back to the island.'

'What island?' asked Hunter.

But Ms Stegg had gone.

'Good luck,' Hunter said to the tops. Then he hit his teleport button, and the tops vanished.

Suddenly, their d-bands all lit up at once. **Buzz!**

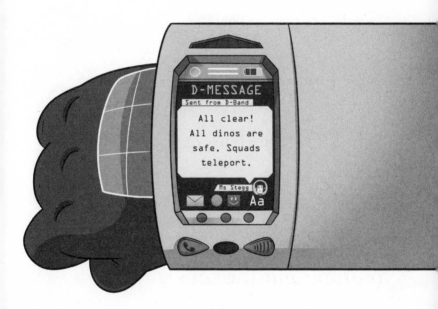

D-MESSAGE

Sent from D-Band

All clear!
All dinos are
safe. Squads
teleport.

Ms Stegg

'Wow, we did it – we got all the dinos!' Charlie said. 'Let's get back to base.'

The team hit their teleport buttons. Seconds later, they found themselves on another island. They were standing on a beach. In front of them was a huge dome. It covered most of the island.

'Ummmmm…this isn't D-Bot Squad base!' said Hunter.

'So, where are we?' asked Charlie.

Ethan pointed to a large steel door in the dome. 'There's a camera with a red light beside this door. Is it taking a photo of us?'

'Screeeech! Aaaaarrk! Growl! Squeak!'

'What was that?' asked Hunter.

Chapter Four

The light on the camera turned green. The big steel door slid open.

Hunter, Charlie and Ethan's mouths dropped wide open.

The three D-Bot Squad members stepped through the door. It closed behind them.

'Duck!' cried Ethan.

Swoosh!

Four pterodactyls swooped over their heads. Then they flew off into some trees.

Was one of those the ptero I caught? thought Hunter.

'Wow!' cried Charlie. She rubbed her eyes. 'Is this for real?'

'Yes, it is, Charlie. Welcome to Dino Corp Island!' said Ms Stegg. She'd come from a steel building nearby. 'This is where all your dinosaurs were teleported to. Come with me. There's lots to show you.'

They followed Ms Stegg into
the steel building. 'This is the
Dino Corp lab,' she said. 'This
is where we found out how to
bring dinosaurs back to life.'

'But how?' asked Charlie.

'We found bones from real dinosaurs,' said Ms Stegg. 'We used the bits inside to grow dinos. First it didn't work, but we kept trying. And we did it!'

'I read about that in my book,' said Hunter. 'But I thought it was only an idea.'

'Not any more,' said Ms Stegg.
'We made lots of dinosaurs.
Then a space rock crashed into
the island.'

'That was on the news,' said
Ethan. 'They said it hit an
empty island, though.'

'Our work has to be a secret,'
said Ms Stegg. 'The space rock
made a hole in the dome.'

'And some dinosaurs escaped to nearby islands?' Charlie guessed.

'That's right,' Ms Stegg said.

'And they took their eggs with them?' Hunter said.

'Right again,' said Ms Stegg. 'But we didn't know that at first. We learnt that from you.'

Hunter blushed. He felt proud.

'Then the eggs began to hatch,'
said Ethan. 'And the baby
dinos grew too fast.'

'But why did they grow so
quickly?' asked Hunter.

'We don't know for sure,' said
Ms Stegg. 'We think the space
rock changed them somehow.'

'Hmmm.' Hunter frowned. He
liked to know things for sure.

Ms Stegg smiled. 'It's okay not to know everything, Hunter. We find out new things by not knowing. We're testing the space rock now. You can help.'

On a bench was a Bunsen burner. In a dish on top was some space rock.

'Bring me that baby strawberry plant, Ethan,' Ms Stegg said.

Ethan put the plant by the
burner.

'Now turn the burner on,
Charlie,' Ms Stegg said.

The rock turned red. Then it
melted. Ms Stegg handed
Hunter a dropper.

'Hunter, drop some melted rock
onto the strawberry plant. Be
careful!'

Hunter did as he was told.

Pop! The strawberries began to grow. **Pop! Pop!**

'They're almost as big as my head!' said Ethan.

'You see?' said Ms Stegg. 'The space rock makes baby things grow up fast. We think that's what happened with the dino-eggs. Luckily, all the eggs are safely back here now.'

'Where are the newest babies now?' asked Charlie.

'I'll show you,' said Ms Stegg.

Hunter, Charlie and Ethan couldn't wait.

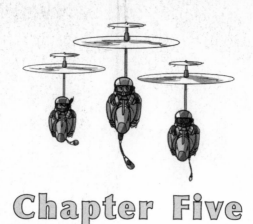

Chapter Five

The D-Bot Squad team walked into the baby-dino room. Their smiles grew bigger and bigger. There were so many cute baby dinos!

'Would you like to feed some babies?' asked Ms Stegg.

'Yes!' the team cried, all at once.

Ms Stegg passed them each a bottle. Hunter fed a baby stegosaurus some moss juice. Charlie fed a baby tops some leaf mush. And Ethan fed a baby ptero some fish slush.

Sluurp! Buuuurp!

'This is so great!' cried Hunter.

Suddenly, a giant ptero
swooped past the window.

Just like at school, thought
Hunter. *No one believed me, but
I was right.*

He looked at Charlie and Ethan
and smiled. *They would have
believed me.*

'Now, I have more to show you,' said Ms Stegg. She pressed a button on her d-band.

The team gasped as an image rose from their own bands.

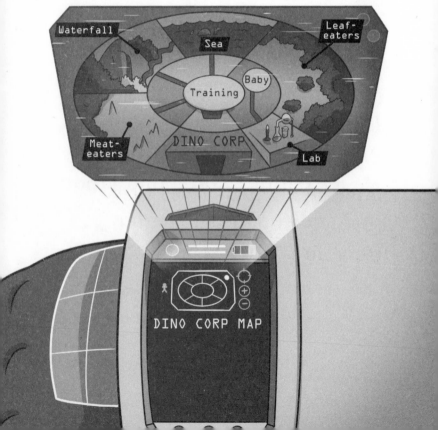

'Use this map to find any dinos you'd like to see,' said Ms Stegg.

'You mean we get to go wherever we want?' Ethan asked.

Charlie couldn't stop grinning. 'I don't know what to pick first.'

But Hunter knew exactly which dino he wanted to see first.

'Have fun!' said Ms Stegg.

Charlie flew down and hovered next to Hunter. 'Can you believe this?' she said. 'I just fed a steg! It ate from my hand.'

Then Ethan showed up. 'I just raced a velociraptor,' he said. 'And I won!'

'I never want to leave this place,' said Hunter.

Then they heard music playing.

'That sounds like the home-time music from school,' said Charlie. 'But it couldn't be…right?'

All three d-bands flashed at the same time.

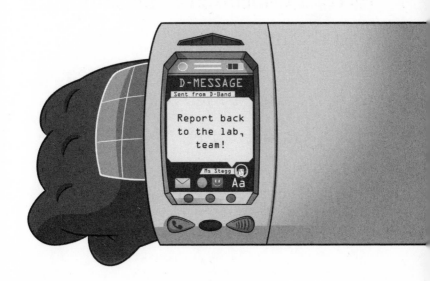

Chapter Six

It was time to leave Dino Corp
Island. Hunter, Charlie and
Ethan stood in front of Ms Stegg.
They were ready to teleport.

'Remember,' said Ms Stegg, 'tell no one about our work.'

Hunter nodded. 'It's top secret.'

'Here is a cover for your d-bands,' said Ms Stegg. 'Wear them at all times. And always be ready.'

'Ready for what?' asked Ethan.

'Anything,' said Ms Stegg.

Hunter, Charlie and Ethan hit the teleport buttons on their d-bands.

Zap!

In a flash, Hunter was back in his school library's dino-cave. He was alone. He was wearing his Book Week costume again. The dino-model he'd been building was still there.

Did all of that really happen?
he wondered.

Hunter came out of the cave.
He scratched his head.

'Great job, Hunter,' said Ms Stegg.

'So, it *was* real?' asked Hunter.

But Ms Stegg only winked.
'Time to go home.'

Hey, thought Hunter, *Charlie goes to my school! And there's Ethan!*

Hunter waved to Charlie. She smiled.

Hunter grinned from ear to ear. 'I have two new best friends!' he said.

Hunter was still grinning when his dad picked him up.

'Hello, dino-hunter,' said his dad. 'How was your day?'

Hunter pulled up his sleeve. He looked at his covered d-band.

'Dad, it was awesome!' he said.